MW01152847

ELMO ASKS
WHY

A First Encyclopedia for Growing Minds

123

SESAME STREET®

ELMO ASKS WHY

A First Encyclopedia for Growing Minds

Written by
Simon Beecroft

Contents

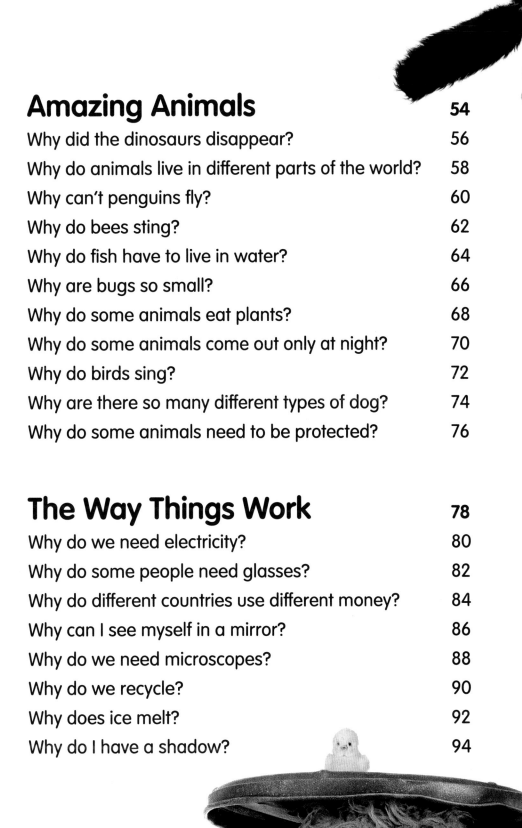

Amazing Animals 54

The Way Things Work 78

Getting Around

The World Around Us

Express Yourself!

Fun and Fitness

CATCH YOU LATER!

Busy People 176

Spectacular Space 194

Welcome!

Elmo is with Elmo's friends, Grover, Big Bird, Cookie Monster, and Abby Cadabby. Elmo has lots of questions about the world, and Elmo bets that you do, too.

When you have questions, the best place to find answers is in an encyclopedia. An encyclopedia is a book that is packed with facts and information. This book is an encyclopedia! Each chapter is about different things, like animals, food, and space.

So why don't you join Elmo and Elmo's friends to find out the answers to lots and lots of questions? Cookie Monster might even learn that the moon is not a cookie!

All About Me

The color of our skin is a part of who we are. We all look **different** in so many ways!

12

Why is my skin the color it is?

Skin is many different colors. Our skin gets its color from **melanin**. We all have melanin in our bodies. It makes the skin on the outside the color that it is.

sunscreen ⇨

We all need to use **sunscreen** in the sun to protect our skin from sunburn.

★ ★ ★ ★ ★ ★ ★ ★ ★

Melanin is also what makes freckles. A lot of sun can give you even more freckles!

Why do I have hair?

You have **more than 100,000** hairs on your head! Your hair keeps your **head warm** and provides a bit of **extra protection** for your skull. That's the long and short of it!

woolly sheep
⇩

About **50 to 100** hairs fall out each day. But don't worry, **new hairs** grow back to replace them.

⁕ ⁕ ⁕ ⁕ ⁕ ⁕ ⁕ ⁕ ⁕ ⁕ ⁕

Hair on animals is called **fur or wool**. It is made of the same material as human hair.

Eyebrows and **eyelashes** are also hair. Eyebrows protect your eyes from sweat from your forehead. Eyelashes stop dust from getting in your eyes.

Why are some people taller than others?

We are all **different heights**. Our bodies are built using a set of **instructions** called **DNA**. Your DNA comes from your birth parents. DNA tells your body how tall it should grow!

A **wall chart** is a good way to see how much you are growing. Mark your height on it **every few months**.

★ ★ ★ ★ ★ ★ ★ ★ ★ ★

You are a little bit **taller in the morning!** Your body stretches out while you sleep and shrinks back down during the day.

GROWING IS GREAT!

⇦ sunflower

Sunflowers are very tall plants. They can grow to more than **twice the height** of an adult!

Big Bird is **MUCH taller** than Elmo!

17

OM NOM NOM NOM!

Your tummy might gurgle **after eating**, too. It's the sound of the food being **mixed around** inside.

Why does my tummy rumble?

Just the smell of food can make your **tummy rumble**. It's the sound of your stomach getting ready to munch yummy food. Think of it as **hunger you can hear**.

⇧
fresh pizza

Tummy rumbles sound louder when your stomach is empty. When you are full, the noises are **muffled** (quieter).

★ ★ ★ ★ ★ ★ ★ ★

Food stays in your tummy for up to **four hours**. It can take **three days** to travel all the way through you.

Why do I get sick?

Sometimes you catch a cold or have an upset stomach. You get sick because of **tiny living things** called **germs**. You can't see germs, but some of them can make you **feel ill**.

Some germs can spread when we **cough** and **sneeze**. Cough or sneeze into the bend in your elbow so your mouth is covered.

When you feel sick, it's important to get plenty of **rest**. Rest helps your body **fight the illness**.

Washing your hands with **soap** and **water** helps to get rid of dirt and germs.

⇧
bar of soap

Doctors help
care for
sick people.
⇩

You have dreams **every night**, whether you remember them or not.

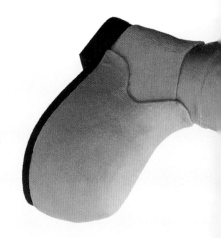

Why do I have dreams?

When you are asleep, your **brain** is still **busy**. No one knows quite why we dream. It may be how your brain sorts through your **thoughts and memories**.

What do you
dream about?

fluffy pillow
⇩

At night, you have lots of **short dreams**. Toward the morning, your dreams tend to be **longer**.

✦ ✦ ✦ ✦ ✦ ✦ ✦ ✦ ✦ ✦ ✦ ✦ ✦

Most people **dream in color**, but some people dream only in **black and white**.

The Count is counting your **senses**. You also can sense temperature and how your tummy feels.

Why are there five senses?

The five main senses are **sight, smell, hearing, taste,** and **touch.** They work together with your brain to help you to understand the world around you.

Fur feels soft to the touch.
⇩

When you touch something, your skin sends a **message** to your brain, telling you what it feels like.

★ ★ ★ ★ ★ ★ ★ ★ ★ ★ ★

Your tongue is covered in thousands of **taste buds,** which recognize flavors.

Sneezes burst out at **high speed** and can travel about as far as the length of **four adult beds!**

⇧
box of
tissues

Why do I sneeze?

Ahh-choooo! When dust or dirt tickles inside your nose or throat, you might need to sneeze. A sneeze is a **sudden burst of air** that clears out your nose.

You can't **sneeze in your sleep** because the part of your brain that controls sneezing is also asleep!

★ ★ ★ ★ ★ ★ ★ ★ ★

Germs from a cold can also make you sneeze.

⇧
sleeping
kittens

Cats sleep for about **15 hours** a day. They are more active at night.

People need different amounts of sleep. Adults need between **seven and nine hours**. Babies sleep the most—up to **18 hours** every day.

Why do I have to sleep?

Sleep is good for you! Sleep **recharges** your body and your brain. After a good sleep, you have lots more **energy** to play and have fun!

Do you sleep on your back, on your tummy, or **on your side,** like Elmo?

29

Why should I brush my teeth?

You use your teeth to **bite and chew** your food. **Brushing your teeth** every day will keep them clean and healthy.

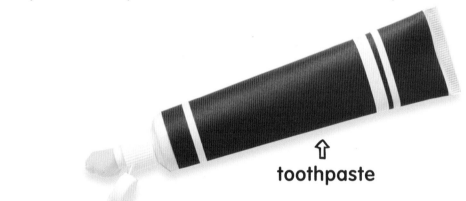

⇧ toothpaste

⇧ toothbrush

Brushing your teeth gets rid of **germs and food** and makes your breath smell fresh.

Have any of your teeth fallen out yet? Your bigger, **adult teeth** will grow to replace them.

Brush your teeth **every morning** and before you go to bed **at night**.

Why do we yawn?

Yawning is your body's way of **waking itself up**. When you yawn, you open your mouth **wide** and breathe in **deeply**. This helps you feel more awake.

sleepy parrots
⇩

yawning dog ⇨

Babies can yawn **before they are born**.

★ ★ ★ ★ ★ ★ ★ ★ ★ ★ ★ ★ ★

Dogs and cats **yawn**, too. Other animals that yawn include birds, reptiles, and even fish!

Fabulous Food

Your body needs **different types of food**, including grains, fruits, vegetables, milk, and meat (or plant-based choices).

You need **three meals a day** and some healthy snacks in between.

⇐ rice is a grain

Why do I need to eat?

Your body needs to **recharge** every day! When you eat, your body gets **energy**. You use the energy to grow, move, play, and have fun!

Dinner time with your friends or family is a special time to enjoy **healthy food** and share **stories**.

Why do I need to drink water?

Glug, glug! It's important to drink water throughout the day. Water is super-healthy and keeps all parts of your body working. So let's **drink up!**

Plants need water, too. ⇨

Your body needs about **four to five cups of water** every day—more if you are running around or if it's hot.

More than half of the **weight of your body** is water!

Drinking **water** and **milk** helps your body to grow. Have you ever tried water flavored with fresh lemon or pineapple slices? Yum!

Tamir and his mom love **gardening** in the Community Center! They **grow vegetables**. Which vegetables are your favorites?

Vegetables contain **vitamins** and **minerals**, which help your body work properly.

Vegetables can be **crunchy** like carrots and **sweet** like corn. How else do vegetables taste?

⇧
quesadilla with vegetables

Why do we eat vegetables?

Cucumber slices. Carrot sticks. Little broccoli "trees." Vegetables are a **tasty** and **healthy food**. They are packed with **nutrition** that your body needs to grow and be healthy.

41

Why is fruit sweet?

Fruits are sweet because they are packed with **natural sugars**. These sugars make the fruit delicious to eat. The seeds, pips, or stones inside a fruit grow into **new plants**.

lemon ⇨

Have you seen **seeds** inside apples and strawberries or a **stone** inside a peach?

✳ ✳ ✳ ✳ ✳ ✳ ✳ ✳ ✳ ✳ ✳ ✳ ✳ ✳ ✳ ✳ ✳ ✳

Not all fruits are sweet. Perhaps you have tasted a **lemon**? Its taste is called **sour**.

Fruits include pears, apples, oranges, and grapes. **Tomatoes** are also a fruit!

A single banana is called a **finger**. A **bunch of bananas** is called a **hand**!

44

Why are bananas curved?

Bananas grow in a very special way!
They start off growing **downward**.
Then they start to **bend
upward** to get more sun.
This makes them **curved**!

BANANAS ARE BRAIN FOOD!

growing bananas ⇩

Banana plants can grow
to the height of **four
refrigerators** stacked
on top of each other!

Bananas contain
vitamin B6, which helps
your brain work well.

whole-grain pancakes ⇨

Why is breakfast important?

Each morning, your body needs to **refuel** for the day ahead. Breakfast helps you to be **healthy** and **active**. Some say it's the most important meal of the day!

⇦ whole-wheat toast

cereal and fruit
⇩

A healthy breakfast improves your **memory** and **concentration**.

Skipping breakfast can make you feel tired, restless, or grouchy.

Breakfast can be hot, like **oatmeal or toast**, or cold, like **cereal or yogurt**. Which do you like best?

OATMEAL IS TOTALLY YUMMY!

Why do I burp?

You put your hand up but it's too late. **"Burp!"**
It's okay. We all burp once in a while. A burp is
just **air**. When you eat or drink, you swallow
extra air and your body pushes it back out.

Lots of animals
make burping
noises, just like you.
Even **bears burp**!

Bubbles in **soda water**
are filled with air. They
can also make you burp!

★ ★ ★ ★ ★ ★ ★ ★ ★ ★

When you burp, it's
polite to put your hand
to your mouth and say
"excuse me."

49

← tomatoes

Tomatoes are red, blueberries are blue... Eating a **rainbow** of different colored foods helps your body get all the nutrition it needs.

Fruits and **vegetables** are packed with healthy vitamins and minerals.

ME EAT HEALTHY FOOD!

⇧ blueberries

Why can't I eat cookies all the time?

Cookies are a **sometimes food**. Your body needs lots of different types of foods, like juicy apples and crunchy carrots, to be healthy. How many other **healthy foods** can you name?

carrots ⇨

⇧
apple

While **cookies** are delicious, they are a **sometimes treat**!

51

Why do I need to wash my hands before I eat?

When you eat a meal, you don't want to also **eat germs**! Washing your hands with soap **kills the germs**. You should also wash your hands after using the bathroom.

Make sure to **wash your hands** after playing outside, after touching pets, and after blowing your nose.

✳ ✳ ✳ ✳ ✳ ✳ ✳ ✳ ✳ ✳ ✳ ✳ ✳

It's also best to give **fruits and vegetables** a quick rinse with water before you eat them.

⇧
strawberries

When you are washing your hands, it should take about the amount of time it takes to sing **"Happy Birthday"** twice.

Amazing Animals

Some dinosaurs were **even bigger** than Big Bird's best friend **Snuffy**!

Why did the dinosaurs disappear?

Dinosaurs were some of the largest animals that roamed the Earth. They lived **millions of years ago**. Scientists think they died out when a **giant rock** from space crashed into Earth.

⇧
T. rex tooth

We know about dinosaurs because we have found their **teeth** and **bones**.

The biggest dinosaurs were as tall as a **five-story building**!

⇧
stegosaurus

57

Frogs live in in ponds and swamps, while **monkeys** prefer to hang out in wet, warm forests.

Why do animals live in different parts of the world?

Every animal needs a **habitat** where they can find the **food they like**. Animals also need **water** and **shelter**.

The place where an animal makes its home is called its **habitat**.

★ ★ ★ ★ ★ ★ ★ ★ ★ ★

Examples of habitats are **deserts**, **forests**, and **oceans**.

A penguin's wings are paddle-like **flippers**. They help them to swim.

Why can't penguins fly?

Most penguins live in **frozen** Antarctica. They have **heavy bodies** and **short wings**, so they can't fly. But they are **brrrr-illiant swimmers**. They can even leap out of the water!

feather

baby penguin ⇨

Penguins **waddle** when they walk. They can also **slide** across the ice on their bellies!

Most baby penguins are born with **fluffy feathers** to keep them warm.

61

Bees fly from **flower to flower**, collecting **nectar.** They turn the nectar into **honey!**

Bees sting with a tiny, pointed **stinger** that sticks out of their tail.

Not all bees can sting. Female honeybees have stingers, but male honeybees are **harmless**.

⇧
stinger

Why do bees sting?

Bees sting only when they are threatened or in danger. Bees are tiny and their **stingers** are their only defense.

discus fish ⇨

⇧
bannerfish

Why do fish have to live in water?

Fish cannot breathe the air like you can. They can breathe only **through water**.

Saltwater fish live in seas and oceans, while **freshwater fish** live in rivers and lakes.

Fish have a waterproof cover called **scales**. They use their **fins** to swim.

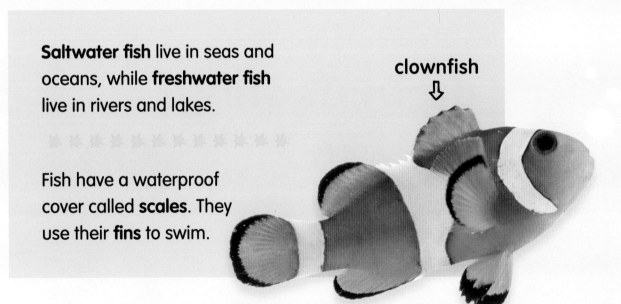
clownfish
⇩

HOW MANY FISH DO YOU SEE?

Fish breathe by taking water **into their mouths**. Then they push it out through holes in their sides called **gills**.

You probably know that **butterflies** and **ladybugs** can fly. But did you know that most **grasshoppers** can also fly?

Why are bugs so small?

Bugs can be teeny tiny, like **mosquitoes and fleas**. Some bugs are a bit bigger, like **crickets and beetles**. Being small helps bugs to hide so that they avoid being eaten by larger animals.

goliath
beetle
⇩

ladybug
⇩

Ladybugs have up to 22 spots—though some have none at all.

★ ★ ★ ★ ★ ★ ★ ★ ★ ★

Goliath beetles are some of the largest bugs. They can be longer than your hand!

ant
⇩

Why do some animals eat plants?

Some animals eat plants because that's what's best for their bodies. These animals are called **herbivores**.

elephant ⇨

snail
⇩

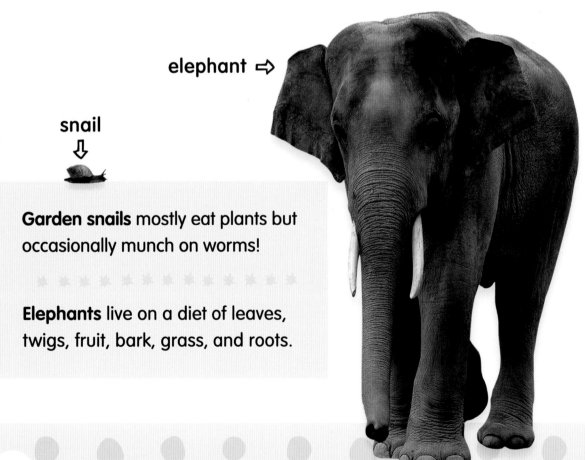

Garden snails mostly eat plants but occasionally munch on worms!

Elephants live on a diet of leaves, twigs, fruit, bark, grass, and roots.

Cows spend most of their time in big green fields eating **lots and lots of grass**. This is known as **grazing**.

Bats can fly in absolute darkness using a special skill called **echolocation**. They make sounds to figure out where they are.

70

Why do some animals come out only at night?

Many animals are **busy at night**, including **bats, owls,** and **badgers**. They like to **hunt at night**, when they can't be seen. Some animals prefer nighttime because it's **cooler** than the day.

⇐ baby owl

Animals who come out at night are called **nocturnal**.

★ ★ ★ ★ ★ ★ ★ ★ ★ ★ ★ ★

Many nocturnal animals have super-strong senses of **smell, sight,** and **hearing**.

Why do birds sing?

Birds "talk" to other birds with **chirps**, **tweets**, and **honks**. Some birds also **sing songs**. These birds are called **songbirds**. They sing to show off and let other birds know they are fit and healthy!

songbird ⇨

Many songbirds sing in the morning. This is known as the **dawn chorus**.

✴ ✴ ✴ ✴ ✴ ✴ ✴ ✴ ✴ ✴

Songbirds learn their songs from their **parents** when they are babies.

Many songbirds have their own **special song**. Listen carefully to hear different songs.

Why are there so many different types of dog?

Dogs can be big, small, fluffy, spotty, sausage-shaped, and more! Long ago, **dogs were wild**. Humans tamed them, either as **pets** or to **do jobs**, such as hunting, rescue, and farmwork.

⇐ Dalmatian puppy

Dalmatians have spotty coats. No two are exactly the same!

✻ ✻ ✻ ✻ ✻ ✻ ✻ ✻ ✻ ✻ ✻ ✻ ✻ ✻

Dogs have a better **sense of smell** than you do. That's how police dogs **sniff out clues**!

There are hundreds of **different breeds** (types) of dog. How many can you name?

75

baby panda ⇨

Endangered animals include **giant pandas, rhinos, tigers,** and **gorillas.**

Protecting endangered animals helps them to **survive.**

Many endangered animals are cared for in **national parks** and **wildlife reserves.**

Why do some animals need to be protected?

Some animals are **endangered**, which means they are in danger of becoming **extinct** (dying out). Instead of hunting these animals and destroying their homes, we must **protect them**.

The Way Things Work

LET'S INVESTIGATE...

Why do we need electricity?

Electricity is a form of **energy** and we need it for lots of things. Almost all machines are **powered by electricity,** including lights and computers.

Batteries store **electrical energy** until it is needed. Many cars are now powered by **electric batteries**.

LED light bulbs last much longer than other types of light bulbs and use less electricity.

⇐ LED light bulb

Electricity travels along wires from a **power station** into your home. How many things can you find in your home that are powered by electricity?

ELMO CAN SEE YOU!

A fun part of wearing glasses is picking the **frames**. Abby is testing out **sparkly sunglasses**!

Why do some people need glasses?

Glasses help people **see better**. Some help people see things that are **far away**. Others help people to do **close-up activities**, like reading.

An **eye exam** tests how well you see. In an eye exam, you read a **chart** with letters or numbers in different sizes.

★ ★ ★ ★ ★ ★ ★ ★ ★ ★ ★ ★

If you can see perfectly, you have what is called **20/20 vision**.

eye exam
⇩

There are many **types of money** in the world. In India, money is called **rupees**, and in Japan, people use **yen**. Can you name any others?

Why do different countries use different money?

Each country has paper money and coins with **different colors** and **designs**. It's part of what makes every country **unique**.

coins
⇩

⇧
paper money

Before money was invented, people would **simply swap** one thing for another!

Some countries use money with the same name. For example, **dollars** are used in the US, Canada, Australia, and some other countries.

Why can I see myself in a mirror?

Mirrors have **smooth** and **shiny surfaces** that reflect light. So, when you look in a mirror, you can see yourself. This is called a **reflection**.

saucepan ⇨

⇦ spoon

Before **mirrors were invented**, people could see their reflection only in water.

✶✶✶✶✶✶✶✶✶✶✶✶✶✶✶✶✶✶✶

Can you see yourself in other things? How about a **spoon** or a **saucepan**?

Mirrors are **flat, shiny,** and **smooth**. They create the best reflections.

snowflake

Snow is made
of **snowflakes**.
No two snowflakes
are exactly alike.

Why do we need microscopes?

Some things are so small that we can see them only with an **instrument** called a **microscope**. A microscope uses special **lenses** to make things look larger.

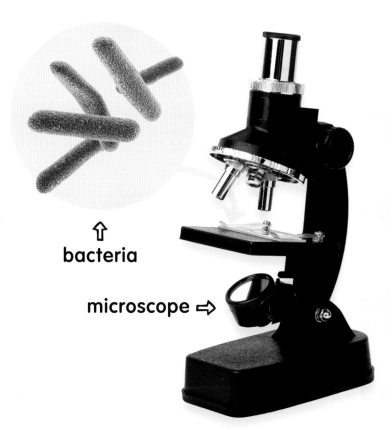

⇧
bacteria

microscope ⇨

The **lenses** in a **microscope** are a bit like the lenses in a pair of glasses—except much more powerful!

With a microscope, we can see tiny things like **snowflakes** and **bacteria**.

Why do we recycle?

Many things that we have finished with can be turned into something else. This is called **recycling**. Plastic bottles can be made into **T-shirts** and recycled paper can become **kitty litter**!

Recycling is important because it **prevents waste** from ending up in our oceans or buried in the ground.

What do you recycle at home? How about **glass, paper, cardboard, metal cans,** or **plastic?**

Whenever you buy food, **check the wrapper** to see if it can be recycled.

Snow is made from frozen water. With snow, you can **make snowballs**. Don't forget your mittens!

Why does ice melt?

Ice is **frozen water**. Water is a **liquid**, but when it freezes it becomes a **solid**. When ice warms up, it melts and becomes a liquid again. **Cool!**

⇐ snowperson

thermometer ⇨

A **thermometer** shows the temperature. Ice melts at **32 degrees Fahrenheit**, which is the same as **zero degrees Celcius**.

A **snowperson** can take many days to **melt completely**.

Why do I have a shadow?

When sunlight or another light shines on you, your body blocks the light. This **makes a shadow**. Your shadow is the same shape as your body.

shadow
puppet
theater
⇩

Outdoors, shadows are longer in the **morning and evening** when the sun is **lower in the sky**.

In a **shadow puppet theater**, you see the shadows of the puppets.

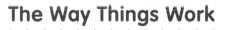

Place a **flashlight** on a chair so that it shines at a wall. Move into the light to see your shadow **on the wall**.

95

Getting Around

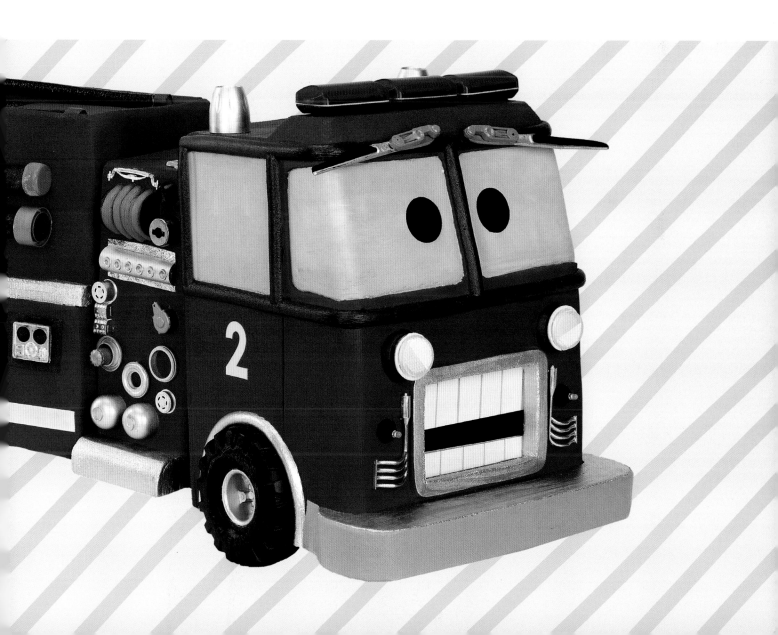

Why do bicycles stay up when people ride them?

The secret to riding a bike is **speed and balance**. It takes practice to ride a bike. You may be a bit wobbly at first. But then—**whoosh**, you're off!

Cycling is three times faster than walking but uses the same amount of energy!

✳ ✳ ✳ ✳ ✳ ✳ ✳ ✳ ✳

Bikes **wobble** when you ride slowly but stay up when you go faster.

bicycle
⇩

ELMO'S COMING!

Elmo has no trouble keeping his tricycle upright. That's because it has **three wheels**!

The **smaller wings** at the back of an airplane help keep it balanced.

Airplane wings are **specially shaped** to help the plane fly.

The first airplane flight took place **120 years ago**.

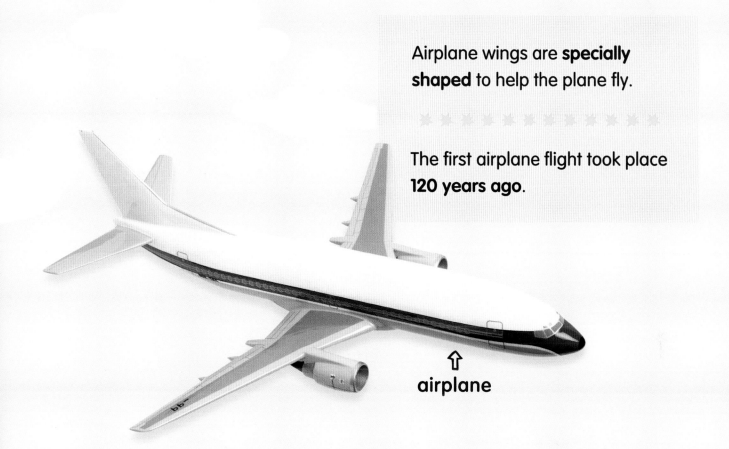

⇧
airplane

Why don't airplanes have flapping wings?

Birds flap their wings to fly. But airplanes are much larger than birds. They need **special engines** to fly. If an airplane's wings flapped, passengers would have a very bumpy ride!

⇧ wheel

Wheels on a bus or car are attached to a pole, called an **axle**. The engine spins the axle around to **turn the wheels**.

✳ ✳ ✳ ✳ ✳ ✳ ✳ ✳ ✳ ✳ ✳ ✳ ✳ ✳ ✳ ✳

Most buses have between **four** and **10 wheels**—or 11 wheels including the steering wheel!

⇦ bus

Why do the wheels on the bus go round and round?

Wheels are very **useful things**! They make it much easier to move something along. **Dragging** a heavy object can be hard work. But **with wheels**, it's much easier!

DON'T MISS THE BUS!

Buses can carry a lot of people, which makes them more **eco-friendly** than cars!

103

Balls and balloons do not
need to be boat-shaped to
float. They float because
they are **filled with air**.

Why do boats float?

Boats are big and heavy, but they don't sink (unless they have a hole in them!). The secret is the shape. Boats have **wide bottoms** and **steep sides**, which help them to float.

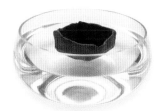

⇧
modeling-clay boat

⇦ **toy sailboat**

A **ball** of modeling clay **won't float**. But the same modeling clay in the **shape of a boat** floats!

Sailboats move when the wind pushes against their sails.

Why do farmers use tractors?

Tractors pull **heavy loads** such as farming tools or trailers. Their big wheels have **deep grooves** in them so that they can move easily in muddy fields.

tractor

Some tractors pull **plows,** which turn over the soil before seeds are planted.

Before the **invention of tractors,** plows were pulled by **horses** and other animals.

Farmers work very hard. They **grow food** to feed people.

ELMO SAYS BE SAFE IN THE CAR!

When a car or any other vehicle stops suddenly, you are pushed forward. This is called **inertia**.

Why do cars have seat belts?

We wear **seat belts** to hold us safely in place in a car or moving vehicle. When the car moves, we do too. The seat belt helps **keep us in place**.

seat belt ⇨

The **first cars** didn't have seat belts. Now, all cars have them.

Seat belts are made from a very strong material called **polyester**.

A **track around the wheels** of some diggers helps them move across rough ground.

The **driver** of a digger operates the **bucket** on the front.

digger ⇩

CAN YOU DIG IT?

Why do we need diggers?

Diggers are used on **construction sites.** They dig holes and lift heavy loads. They can do the work much faster than a **spade**!

Front loaders have a scoop at the front for pushing heavy materials.

Wes and his dad are talking about **helicopters**. Have you ever seen a helicopter flying above you?

Unlike an airplane, a helicopter can fly **straight up** and **hover**.

★ ★ ★ ★ ★ ★ ★ ★ ★ ★ ★ ★ ★ ★

Sometimes, helicopters are used to **rescue people** from disasters such as fires, floods, and earthquakes.

helicopter ⇨

Why do helicopters have a propeller on top?

A **propeller** is a device with two or more blades that spin at high speed. The blades make the helicopter **move**. Propellers are also used on ships and some airplanes.

⇐ fire helmet

Why are fire trucks red?

Wee-woo-wee-woo! Fire trucks and fire engines need to get quickly to a fire. Being **bright red** helps them stand out. **Other cars** can see them and let them pass.

While most fire trucks are **red**, some are yellow, green, or white!

⇧ fire truck

Fire engines carry hoses for putting out fires. **Fire trucks** carry long ladders on the top.

Firefighters wear **special clothing** that protects them from the heat when they are fighting a fire.

ELMO'S FAVORITE COLOR IS RED!

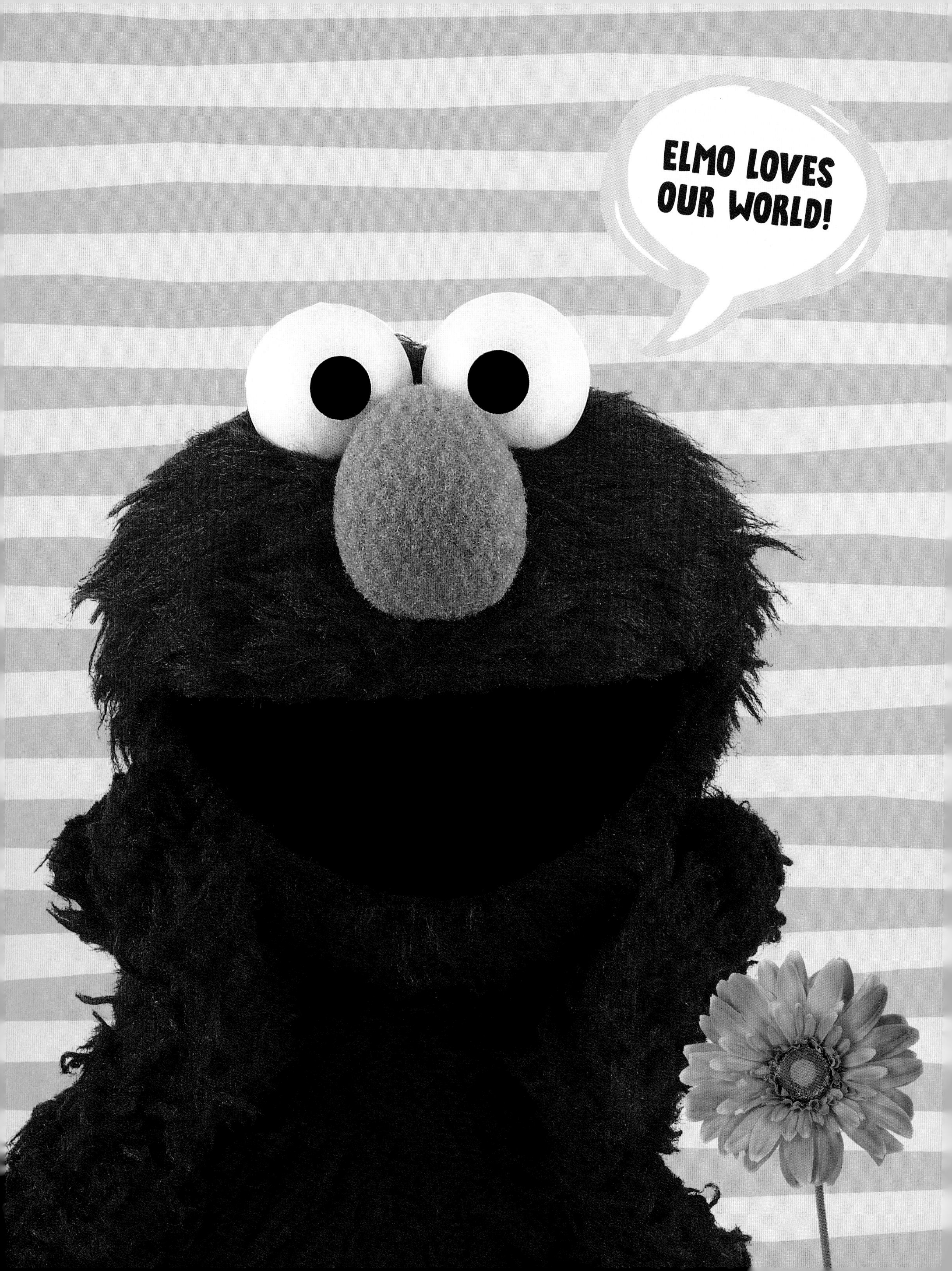
ELMO LOVES OUR WORLD!

The World Around Us

In spring and summer, most flowers are **in bloom**. Flowers make Rudy happy!

Why do we have seasons?

It takes a year for the Earth to **travel around the sun**. As we do so, the amount of sunlight we get each day changes because of the Earth's position. This causes the **different seasons**.

⇧ spring ⇧ summer ⇧ fall ⇧ winter

Deciduous trees blossom in spring and grow leaves in summer. In fall, their leaves turn brown and drop off. In winter, they are bare.

* * * * * * * * * * * * * * * *

Evergreen trees, such as fir trees, stay green all year round.

⇧ fall leaves

119

Why does it rain?

Clouds are made of **tiny droplets of water**. These droplets join together to make bigger droplets. When the droplets get too large and heavy, they **fall to the ground** as rain.

raindrop ⇨

clouds ⇩

People, animals, and **plants** need water to live.

✳ ✳ ✳ ✳ ✳ ✳ ✳ ✳ ✳ ✳ ✳ ✳ ✳

Rain, snow, sleet (a mix of rain and snow), and **hail** (little balls of ice) can all fall from clouds. This is called **precipitation**.

Rain is made of big droplets of water. Smaller droplets are called **drizzle**.

It's safe to draw the sun, but you should **never stare directly** at it.

The sky is **not always blue**. On a rainy day, it is gray. At sunset or sunrise, the sky can be orange and red.

★ ★ ★ ★ ★ ★ ★ ★ ★

If you look up at the sky, you're looking at Earth's **atmosphere**!

Why is the sky blue?

Sunlight is made up of all the **colors of the rainbow**. Most of these colors pass straight through **Earth's atmosphere**, except for blue light, which is why the sky looks blue!

BLUE SKIES ARE COOL!

Look up in the **dark sky** and count how many **stars** you can see!

Why does it get dark at night?

The Earth is **spinning all the time**. At night, the side of the Earth that you are on is away from the sun. The sunlight cannot reach you, so it **becomes dark**.

⇧
Earth

As your part of the Earth turns **toward the sun**, it begins to get light. This is daybreak.

When it is **daytime** where you are, it is nighttime on the other side of the world.

← cosmos flower

sunflower ⇩

Why are flowers so colorful?

Flowers are **brightly colored** to attract insects like bees and butterflies. Insects **pollinate** the flowers, which is how flowers **grow seeds** and make new flowers.

⇧ daisy

Flowers must **swap pollen** with each other to grow seeds. Insects carry pollen from one flower to the next.

Pollen is a **yellow powder** found in the middle of flowers.

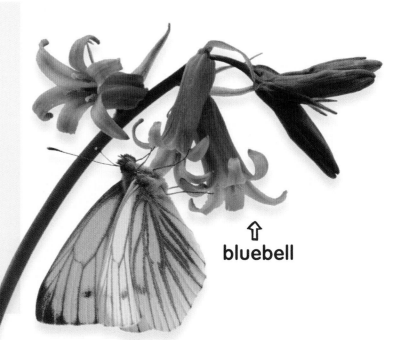

⇧ bluebell

The most **colorful part** of a flower is its petals. Petals can be many different shapes.

rainbow ⇨

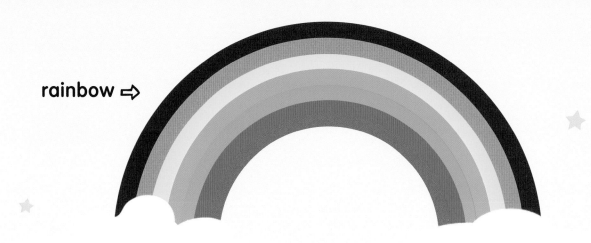

One way to remember
the colors in the rainbow
is ROY G BIV: red, orange,
yellow, green, blue,
indigo, and violet.

WOW!

Why do rainbows appear in the sky?

Next time it rains and the sun is shining at the same time, look for **a rainbow**. A rainbow appears when sunlight shines through drops of water.

colors ⇨

Light is made of **many colors**. When the sun shines through a raindrop, the water **splits the light** into all of its colors.

★ ★ ★ ★ ★ ★ ★ ★ ★ ★ ★ ★ ★

You can **make a rainbow**! Place a piece of cardboard with a slit in it next to a glass of water on a sunny day.

129

THE EARTH IS A GIANT JIGSAW PUZZLE!

Each year, **millions of earthquakes** happen, but most are so **small** people don't even feel them.

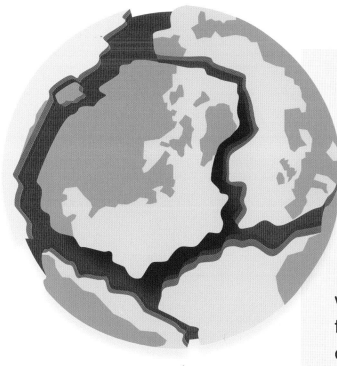

⇧
Earth's plates

The Earth is made from moving pieces of rock called **plates** that fit together like a jigsaw puzzle.

★ ★ ★ ★ ★ ★ ★ ★ ★

Earthquakes happen when **two plates** rub together or bump up against each other.

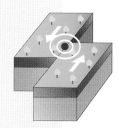

Why are there earthquakes?

Earthquakes happen when the earth **rumbles** and **shakes**. Mostly they are harmless, but sometimes the movement cracks the ground.

⇧
road after an earthquake

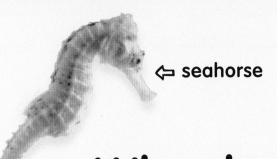
← seahorse

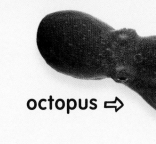
octopus ⇒

Why does Earth have oceans?

Billions of years ago, the Earth was **boiling hot**—all the rocks were so hot they gave off steam. As **the planet cooled**, this steam became all the water in the oceans!

jellyfish
⇓

← sea turtle

coral
⇓

Oceans cover more than **two-thirds** of the Earth's surface. Many animals and plants live in oceans.

✵ ✵ ✵ ✵ ✵ ✵ ✵ ✵ ✵ ✵ ✵

Coral looks like a colorful plant, but it is actually an animal!

The **five oceans** are the Pacific, the Atlantic, the Indian, the Southern, and the Arctic Oceans.

Why does the wind blow?

Wind is **moving air**. When air flows over warm land, it heats up and rises. This leaves room for cooler air to flow in. The **flowing air** is called wind.

A **light wind** is called a breeze. A **stronger wind** is called a gale. A weather vane shows which way the wind is blowing.

✵ ✵ ✵ ✵ ✵ ✵ ✵ ✵ ✵

Some activities need wind, such as surfing, sailing, and kite flying.

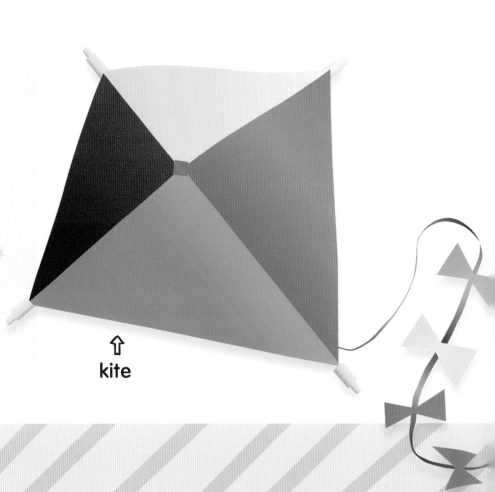

⇧
kite

Sometimes the wind can even blow in **more than one direction** at the same time!

Why is it important to take care of the Earth?

The Earth is **our home**, and it is the only one we have. So, just like we take care of the home we live in, we must respect **the Earth**, too.

Our planet provides **everything we need**: food and water, air to breathe, and materials for making things.

There are many ways to **take care** of the Earth. For example, by reducing, reusing, and recycling plastic waste.

Recycling is good for the Earth!

Just like Cookie Monster, you can use **scrap paper** to make cards.

Express Yourself!

DO YOUR OWN THING!

KONNICHIWA
(Japanese)

HOLA
(Spanish)

HALLO
(German)

SALAM
(Arabic)

Why are there so many languages?

All around the world, people have invented their own languages. In total, humans speak more than **7,000 different languages**!

One of the **rarest languages** is Njerep, spoken by only four people in Nigera, Africa.

✳ ✳ ✳ ✳ ✳ ✳ ✳ ✳ ✳ ✳

English is the most **widely spoken language**, followed by Mandarin, the official language of China.

BOOKS COME IN MANY LANGUAGES!

140

Speaking **another language** is a wonderful tool to learn about your **own culture** and learn about **other cultures**.

141

A harmonica makes sounds when you **blow into it**. Banjos and violins have strings, which are **plucked or bowed**.

⇐ banjo

harmonica
⇓

violin
⇓

Why do musical instruments make different sounds?

Musical instruments are made from **various materials,** such as wood or metal. They are played in different ways, too, so each one **sounds unique.**

One musical instrument sounds different from another, even when both play the **same note.**

In an orchestra, tubas play **low notes** and flutes play **high notes.**

tuba ⇩

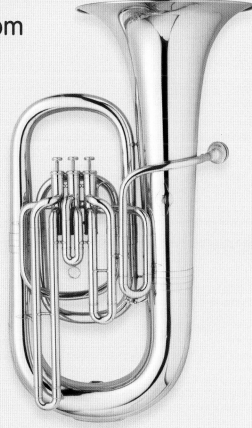

flute ⇩

143

⇦ chisel

Why are some sculptures made of stone?

Stone is a **hard material** that can be made into a sculpture using special tools. Sculptures can also be made of other materials, such as wood, but stone **lasts the longest**.

People on an island called **Easter Island** made huge stone sculptures of heads.

✳ ✳ ✳ ✳ ✳ ✳ ✳ ✳

When carving stone, the sculptor chips away with tools, like a **chisel and hammer**.

Easter ⇨
Island
statue

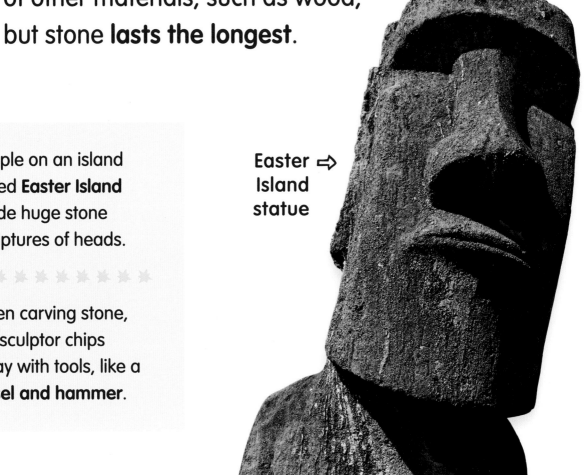

HELLO, BIG SCULPTURE!

Sculptures are solid, or 3-D, **works of art**. They can be large or small!

⇐ *Sunflowers* by Vincent van Gogh

Some artists create art for museums. Other artists **produce art** for books, movies, websites, and many other places.

✳ ✳ ✳ ✳ ✳ ✳ ✳ ✳ ✳ ✳

The **largest museum** in the world is the Louvre in Paris, France.

Why is there art in museums?

Many precious **paintings and sculptures** are kept in museums, where they are carefully taken care of. You can go visit them and **take a look**!

Why don't you make some **art of your own**? Maybe one day it will be in a museum!

Artists often **mix their colors** on a wooden board, called a palette.

Why does mixing some colors make other colors?

Red, blue, and yellow are called **primary colors**. You can mix any two of these colors to make a **secondary color**. For example, if you mix blue and yellow, you make green.

⇧
mixing paints

If you mix red and blue, you get **purple**. Red and yellow make **orange**!

You can use **black and white** to make new colors, too. Mix white and red to get **pink**!

⇦ twinkling lights at Diwali

⇧ menorah

Why do people celebrate holidays?

Around the world, people celebrate **special days**, called holidays or festivals. Holidays bring people together and often involve **special activities** or **traditions**.

⇦ festive gifts

At **Hanukkah**, people light candles on the menorah. **Diwali** is also known as "Divali," "Dipawali," or "the Festival of Lights."

Many people give gifts for **Christmas**. **Eid al-Fitr** marks the completion of the holy month of **Ramadan** and the end of fasting.

Lunar New Year celebrates the beginning of a new year according to the lunar calendar. **Kwanzaa** celebrates African heritage, tradition, and culture. Which holidays do you celebrate?

Reading stories can give you **new thoughts** and **ideas** and take you on **exciting adventures** in your imagination.

Why do people tell stories?

For thousands of years, people have **told stories**. Through stories, you learn about the world and feel the **emotions** of the characters.

genie lamp
⇩

Reading and telling stories is a great way to pass down **traditions** and **cultures**.

✳ ✳ ✳ ✳ ✳ ✳ ✳ ✳ ✳ ✳ ✳

Fairy tales are stories about magical people and imaginary creatures.

⇐ **princess grouchy**

153

There are many styles of dancing. **Bollywood dancers** tell a story using hand movements.

* * * * * * * *

Ballroom dancing is a popular hobby and a competitive sport!

ballroom ⇨
dancers

⇧
Bollywood dancer

Why do people dance?

You hear a beat, so you tap your feet.
Next thing you know, **you're dancing**!
Dancing is a way to **express yourself**
and communicate your emotions.

DANCING IS FUN!

Dancing is **good for you**!
You can release your energy
and show your excitement.

The sound you get from a **tap shoe** depends on how hard you hit the floor and which part of your foot you use.

Why do tap shoes make noise?

Tap dancers use their shoes to **tap the floor** and make noise. The sound is made by **metal pieces** attached to the bottom of the shoes, on the heel and toe.

tap shoes
⇩

Some **tap dancers** dance without music. They create their own "music" through the sounds of their taps.

★ ★ ★ ★ ★ ★ ★ ★ ★ ★

Tap dancing is a great way to improve **balance** and **coordination**.

Fun and Fitness

Have you ever tried **jumping rope**? It takes practice, but it is great exercise.

A HOP, SKIP, AND A JUMP!

Why is exercise good for me?

Exercise keeps you **fit and healthy**. It makes your muscles stronger and even helps you to **sleep better**. Also, it's fun!

FLYING KEEPS ME FIT!

jump in! ⇨

There's so many **fun ways** to exercise, from swimming to playing football or basketball. Even dancing is exercise!

★ ★ ★ ★ ★ ★ ★ ★ ★ ★ ★ ★ ★ ★

Together with your friends and family, you can go for **walks** or a **bike ride**.

Why do I get out of breath when I run?

Running uses a lot more energy than walking. Your body is working harder, so it's easy to get **out of breath**. Your body needs large amounts of **oxygen** when it is running.

Running is not just about **winning a race**. It is also about enjoying yourself.

lungs ⇨

Your lungs are inside your chest. They take in a gas called oxygen from the air.

When you run, there is a point when both your feet are **off the ground** at the same time!

I AM A LITTLE OUT OF BREATH!

baseball ⇨

bowling ball ⇨

⇧
soccer ball

Why are balls different shapes and sizes?

Balls are made for different sports. Basketballs are **round and bouncy**. Footballs are oval-shaped so they are easier to **carry** and **throw**.

CATCH YOU LATER!

football
⇩

tennis ball
⇩

Basketballs used to be brown. They are now orange because orange is **easier to see**.

A **bowling ball** is heavy so it can knock down bowling pins. The stitches in a **baseball** help it to spin in the air.

When **tennis** was first played, players used their hands to hit the ball!

165

Some slides are **straight**. Others are **curved**. Slides at water parks let you plunge into the water!

Some slides are **tube-shaped** and you go down inside!

playground slide
⇩

Why do I go down the slide so fast?

Wheee! Going down a slide is super-fun. A force called **gravity** is what makes you slide down. When the slide is **smooth and dry**, you'll slide even faster!

When your bare legs touch the slide, they cause **friction**, which is the force that makes you go slower.

⇧
slide

When you stop spinning,
your brain takes a moment
to **catch up**. This is why you
get a **dizzy feeling**!

Why do I get dizzy when I spin around?

Your ears are really amazing. They **help you hear** and **help you balance**. When you spin around, the parts of your ear that help you balance move fast as well and can make you **dizzy**.

spinning top
⇩

Special parts of your ears, called your **inner ear**, send messages to your brain when you move.

★ ★ ★ ★ ★ ★ ★ ★ ★ ★

When a **spinning top** stops spinning, it **wobbles**, and we do too!

169

Team sports like **football** or **soccer** teach you to trust and rely on your teammates.

Why do people play team sports?

Playing in a team is fun and a great way to **make friends**. You learn skills like **working together**. When your team loses, it's important to be a **good sport**!

trophy ⇨

ice hockey ⇨

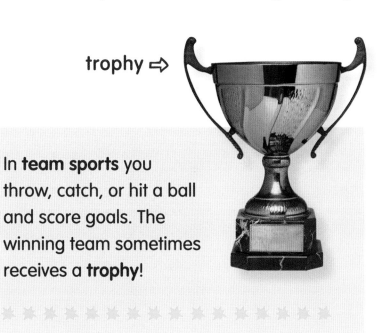

In **team sports** you throw, catch, or hit a ball and score goals. The winning team sometimes receives a **trophy**!

In **ice hockey**, teams score goals by hitting a rubber disk called a puck with flat sticks.

SAFETY FIRST!

Why do I wear a helmet when I ride a bicycle?

Your head is **precious**. It **contains your brain**, which you need for everything you do! A helmet **protects your head** if you have a fall.

People also wear helmets to **play sports** such as football and ice hockey. **Motorcycle riders** also wear helmets.

Other people who wear helmets include **rock climbers**, **horseback riders**, and **skiers**.

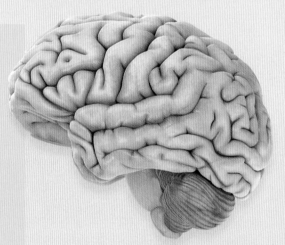

⇧ brains are soft and squishy!

⇐ football helmet

⇑
ice hockey helmet

Bike helmets have a layer of **special foam** inside that cushions your head.

With yoga, you can learn all sorts of twisty, stretchy positions, like **child's pose** and **washing machine pose**!

Yoga is one of the **oldest exercises** in the world. It is over **5,000 years** old!

child's pose
⇩

⇧
washing machine pose

Why do some people do yoga?

When you do **yoga**, you learn how to breathe and move your body into **special positions**. It keeps you **fit** and can help you **feel calm**.

People who are **skilled at yoga** can hold each position for a long time.

Busy People

Why do people have different jobs?

A dentist's job is to **check your teeth**, and an astronaut's job is to **blast off** into space. There are so many **jobs** that need to be done!

People train to do their jobs. For example, **veterinarians** must learn how to care for many different **animals**.

Postal workers deliver mail to people's homes. What job would **you** like to have?

One of the **loudest jobs** is being the drummer in a band! One, two, three—**hit it!**

ME PLAY COOKIE ROCK!

A doctor uses a **stethoscope**
to listen to your heartbeat
and your breathing.

Why do people visit doctors?

You visit a doctor for **check-ups** to keep you healthy. When you feel **sick**, the doctor will find out how to make you **feel better**.

⇧
thermometer

⇦ **stethoscope**

Doctors study **medicine**, which is the science of keeping people healthy. Some become **experts** in particular parts of the body, such as **the heart**.

Doctors use some **special tools**, such as a **thermometer** to check your temperature.

wheat

barley

oats

Farmers **sow seeds** in the fields, which grow into plants that are made into foods like bread.

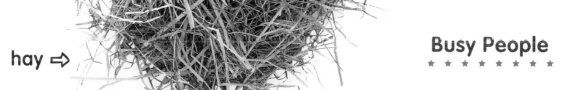

hay ⇨

Why does a farmer get up so early?

Cock-a-doodle doo! It's not even sunrise and farmers are **already up**! First, they milk the cows and feed hay to the animals. Then, they **drive the tractor!**

potatoes
⇩

pig
⇩

Some farms grow crops in the ground, including **vegetables** such as potatoes and corn.

★ ★ ★ ★ ★ ★ ★ ★ ★ ★

Many different **kinds of animals** are found on farms, including cows, sheep, pigs, goats, chickens, horses, geese, and turkeys.

screwdriver
⇩

⇧
saw

Why does a builder have so many tools?

Builders and **construction workers** build houses, bridges, roads, and much more. They use many types of tool, and each tool does **a different job**.

tape measure ⇨

Screwdrivers are for putting in screws and **saws** are for cutting. **Tape measures** are used to measure the length of things.

⇦ screw

toolbox
⇩

Builders often carry their tools around in a **toolbox** or on a special belt around their waist.

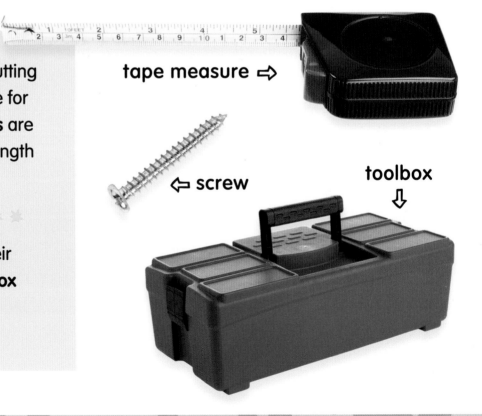

SO MANY TOOLS TO USE!

One end of a hammer is for **hammering in nails** and the other end is for pulling them out!

Some bakers work at night so that people can have **fresh, warm bread** and pastries in the morning.

ME MIXING DOUGH!

Why do some people work at nighttime?

Many people work at **nighttime**. Cleaners work in offices while **no one else is there**. Delivery drivers transport things to **stores**. Even some restaurants are open all night!

Doctors and nurses work **at night** in hospitals. They care for sick or injured patients.

★ ★ ★ ★ ★ ★ ★ ★ ★ ★

Police officers patrol at night, and **firefighters** are ready to respond to emergencies.

Teachers enjoy hearing all
about what you know, too.
So **raise your hand**...

Why does my teacher know so much?

Teachers go to **school** to learn to be teachers. They study **English**, **math**, **science**, and more. Then they share their **love of learning** with you!

⇐ guitar

books
⇩

Teachers teach many skills, such as how to **read**, how to play a **musical instrument**, or how to do **karate**!

★ ★ ★ ★ ★ ★ ★ ★ ★ ★ ★ ★ ★ ★

You will have many **teachers** in your life who will teach you many different things.

Why do some people travel for work?

Most adults go somewhere to work, such an **office**, **store**, or **factory**. But sometimes they need to travel to **other places** to work, too.

Airline pilots and **airplane crews** travel for work—because traveling IS their work! Sometimes, they fly all the way to the **other side of the world** and back again!

✶ ✶ ✶ ✶ ✶ ✶ ✶ ✶ ✶

Actors often travel to different locations when they are shooting scenes for a **movie or TV show**.

actors
⇩

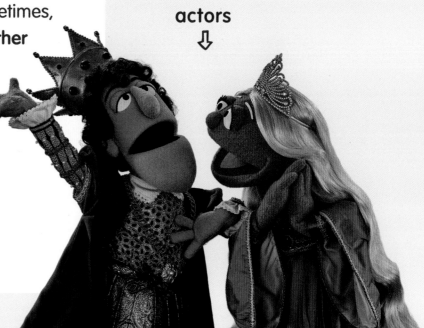

SAY CHEESE!

Photographers often travel the world looking for great shots.

191

Some people raise money for a good cause by **baking cakes** and selling them.

Volunteering for a good cause makes people **feel happy**. How could you help your community?

Why do some people volunteer for good causes?

People who volunteer **don't get paid**. They just want to help others out and support **a good cause**, such as cleaning up the park!

There are so many good causes, including **planting trees** or **flowers** in the local community or **raising money** for your school.

Grover is donating a plant.
⇩

Spectacular
Space

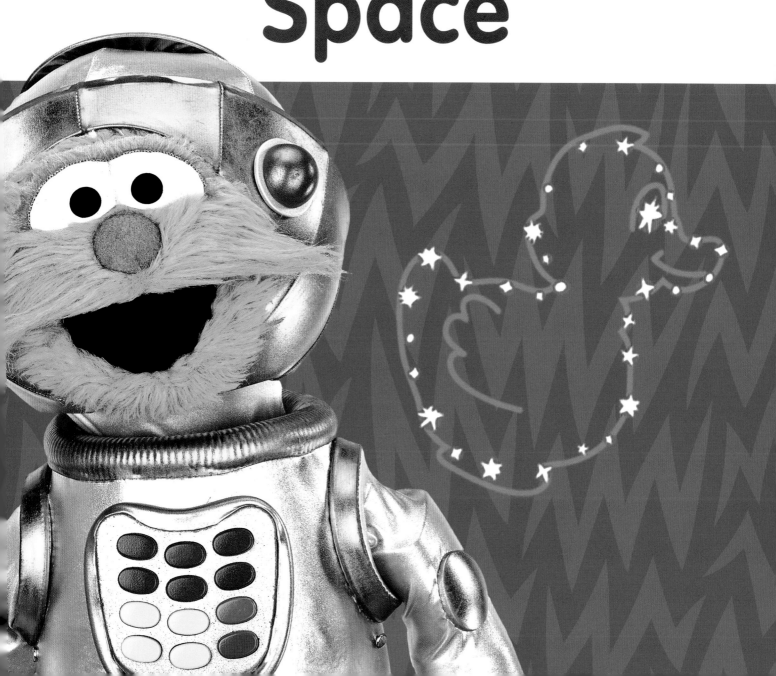

Sometimes the sun disappears in the day! This is called **an eclipse,** and it happens when the moon is in between the sun and Earth.

The sun is a **spinning ball of hot gas** called a **star**. The sun gives out lots of light and heat.

the sun ⇨

Why can't I see the sun at night?

We see the sun in the sky **during the day**. But the Earth is spinning around. So at night, the sun is on the **other side** of the Earth from us!

When it gets dark, your brain knows it's time to **snuggle up** with your favorite toy.

Why do we have a moon?

The moon **shines brightly** in the night sky. Billions of years ago, a smaller planet **hit the Earth** and all the bits of rock from the explosion joined together to make the moon!

The moon is a **ball of rock**. It is about a quarter of the size of the Earth. Its surface has **mountains** and **huge craters** on it.

✳ ✳ ✳ ✳ ✳ ✳ ✳ ✳ ✳ ✳

Since 1969, when humans first **landed on the moon**, **12 people** have walked on the surface!

⇧
moon rock

The moon shines brightly, but it doesn't make its own light. It **reflects light** from the sun.

There are more stars
in the sky than **all the
grains of sand** on **all
the beaches** on Earth!

telescope ⇨

Using a **telescope** will make the stars look closer. You can also see planets.

The light from stars takes **many years** to reach Earth. So when you look at the stars, you are looking back in time!

Why do stars shine?

Stars look like **tiny twinkling lights** in the night sky. But actually they are huge balls of **hot, burning gas**. Our sun is the closest star to the Earth.

Why do things float in space?

In space, things are a little different than here on Earth. Things can float around in space, even **upside down**! The feeling of floating is called **weightlessness**.

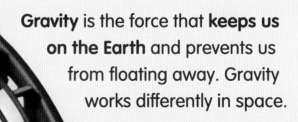

Gravity is the force that **keeps us on the Earth** and prevents us from floating away. Gravity works differently in space.

When a **roller coaster** shoots downward, your body feels like it's floating in the air!

Astronauts have to **train** and **prepare** for weightlessness in space.

Why do astronauts wear special suits in space?

In space, there is no oxygen to breathe, so astronauts wear **spacesuits**. These special suits protect astronauts and give them air to breathe.

It takes about **45 minutes** for an astronaut to put on their spacesuit!

✷ ✷ ✷ ✷ ✷ ✷ ✷ ✷ ✷ ✷ ✷ ✷ ✷ ✷ ✷ ✷ ✷ ✷ ✷ ✷

Spacesuits are fitted with special tubes and bags so that astronauts can **go to the bathroom** without taking off their suit.

⇧
spacesuit

The universe is **everything that is in space,** including all the **stars** and **planets!**

ARE THERE COOKIES IN SPACE?

Why is the universe so big?

The universe is so big because it is **expanding** (growing bigger) every second. This has been going on for around **14 billion years** and it is still growing today!

solar system
⇩

The Earth is one of eight planets in our **solar system**. All eight planets **orbit** (rotate around) the sun.

★ ★ ★ ★ ★ ★ ★ ★ ★ ★

There is also a **dwarf planet** in our solar system called **Pluto**. It is smaller than our moon.

Right now, people are living on a big spacecraft called the **International Space Station.** They are doing experiments and learning about space.

⇧ International Space Station

Hubble ⇦ Space Telescope

SPACE IS AMAZING!

↑
space shuttle

space rocket
⇓

Why do humans go into space?

Three... two.... one... liftoff! Astronauts travel into space on board **powerful rockets** and **space shuttles**. They go to space to learn about the planets, stars, moons, and lots more!

The first person to **walk on the moon** was an American named Neil Armstrong in 1969.

★ ★ ★ ★ ★ ★ ★ ★ ★ ★ ★ ★ ★ ★ ★

The **Hubble Space Telescope** travels around in space and takes amazing pictures.

Why doesn't Earth travel through space like a ship?

The Earth IS traveling through space! We travel **around the sun** in a big, wide circle. It takes **365 days** (one year) to go all the way around!

sun and Earth ⇨

You can't feel it, but the Earth is **traveling around the sun** at about 18 miles (30 kilometers) per second. That's fast!

✳ ✳ ✳ ✳ ✳ ✳ ✳ ✳ ✳ ✳ ✳ ✳ ✳ ✳ ✳ ✳

As the Earth travels around the sun, the planet is also **spinning**.

Earth ⇨

The sun's powerful force of **gravity** keeps the Earth spinning around it without flying away!

Glossary

air
All living things need air. It is a mixture of gases, including oxygen. The air that surrounds the Earth is known as the atmosphere.

Anarctica
Antarctica is the icy region around the South Pole.

atmosphere
The atmosphere is the air that surrounds the Earth.

bug
Bugs are insects or small crawling animals—for example, bees, ants, and spiders.

dinosaur
Dinosaurs were prehistoric animals that inhabited our planet for more than 150 million years. The word *dinosaur* means "terrible lizard."

DNA
DNA is the stuff that makes everyone unique, from the shape of your face to the color of your eyes. It is like a set of instructions for making YOU.

energy
Energy is another word for power. Energy makes things move and makes machines work. Energy also makes living things grow.

force
A force is a push or a pull. When you jump on a trampoline, a force called gravity makes you come down again.

friction

When two objects slide over one another, a force called friction slows them down.

galaxy

A galaxy is a group of stars, clouds of gas, and bits of dust. There are billions of galaxies in the universe.

gas

A gas floats around freely, changing shape all the time. A gas is not a liquid or a solid.

gravity

Gravity is the force that stops us from floating off the Earth.

germ

Germs are tiny living things that can cause disease. They are so small that they creep into our bodies without being noticed.

habitat

A habitat is a place where animals live and can find water, food, and a place to sleep.

inertia

Inertia is the jolting feeling you have when a vehicle stops and when a vehicle begins to move.

LED

A light-emitting diode (LED) is a device that produces light from electricity. LEDs last a long time and do not break easily.

lens

A lens is a piece of glass that is curved on one or both sides. When you look though a lens, objects appear bigger or smaller.

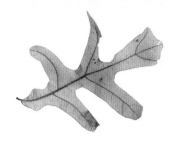

liquid

A liquid is a substance that can be poured. Liquids become solid when they freeze. When they heat up, they becomes a gas called steam.

material

A substance used to make something is called a material. For example, a chair can be made from wood, which is a material.

melanin

A natural substance in your body that gives your skin its color.

mineral

Like vitamins, minerals help your body grow and stay healthy. Our bodies use minerals for many things, from building strong bones to keeping our hearts working properly.

nectar

Nectar is a sugary liquid made by plants. Nectar attracts pollinating animals such as bees and butterflies.

pollen

Pollen is a powder that plants make so they can form seeds. New plants then can grow from the seeds.

pollination

Pollination is the way that flowers make more flowers. Insects, birds, bats, and the wind take pollen between flowers, which means the plants can make seeds and create more plants.

recycling

Recycling means making trash into something new. We can recycle paper, cardboard, plastic, metal, and many other materials.

scale

A fish scale is a small, hard plate that grows out of the skin of a fish. Scales can be different shapes, sizes, and colors. Scales help to protect the fish.

season

The year is divided up into seasons with different types of weather. Many parts of the world have four seasons called spring, summer, fall (autumn), and winter.

solid

A solid is an object that keeps its shape, like a saucepan or an apple. A solid is not a gas or a liquid, but a liquid can become a solid when it freezes.

space

Space and outer space are different. Earth sits in space. Outer space is everything outside of Earth's atmosphere.

substance

A substance is the material from which something is made. Substances can be seen, touched, or measured.

telescope

A telescope makes things appear bigger, which is useful when looking at things that are very far away.

universe

The universe is what we call everything that exists.

vitamin

Vitamins are substances that humans need so that we can grow and be healthy. Very few vitamins are made in the human body. We get most of the vitamins we need from food.

Index

Index

GUIDE FOR GROWN-UPS

Celebrate the questions young children ask!

These seemingly endless inquiries are very important to learning. They reflect a growing curiosity about the world. Questions are how children fill their knowledge gap and instill a love of learning. Will you always know the answers? Perhaps not, but that is where *Elmo Asks Why* can help. This important encyclopedia provides answers to some of the most common questions asked by young children.

Read often and early!

Enjoying books with preschoolers is a powerful bridge between oral language and emerging literacy. When conversations are paired with books, children begin making important connections between listening/speaking and reading/writing. Allow them to select their books and then discuss interesting vocabulary during the read-aloud. And remember to be patient when young children ask to hear a book over and over again. Revisiting the same title nurtures a lifelong love of reading.

The questions children ask

Young children ask many questions as they explore and make sense of the world. Posing queries is exactly what we want them to do! Developmentally, children usually ask "why" questions before other "wh" questions. New research assures us that the "whys" are not meant to exasperate parents and caregivers. They are genuine attempts to learn. Providing age-appropriate and accurate answers to "why" questions helps preschoolers make important connections between what they know and new information.

Questioning as conversation

It is not your imagination—young children do ask lots of questions. It's wonderful that your child is asking questions. Support their curiosity and sense of wonder! Do not let yourself become overwhelmed if you don't know the answer. Simply explain that you don't know and model your own love of learning. Respond with suggestions such as "I am not sure, where do you think we might find that answer?" or "why don't we find the answer together?"

Where to go next

After enjoying *Elmo Asks Why*, continue learning by asking and researching additional questions. After reading about a topic in the encyclopedia, swap "why" with more complex question stems such "how do" or "how might." For example, after reading about why penguins can't fly, ask "how do other animals move?" Or after learning why some sculptures are made of stone, try "how might you make a sculpture?"

Question suggestions

Below are a few more question stems sure to promote lively discussions and additional reading.

> **Which can? Why would?**
> **How would? Where might?**
> **Who can?**

Consider creating an extension of the encyclopedia by writing paragraphs together that answer these more challenging questions. Then, bring the concepts to life with your child's art or photos. Before long, your family can read both *Elmo Asks Why* and _____'s (your child's name) *Book of Facts!*

Drawing the answers

After reading all or part of the encyclopedia, invite your preschooler to respond to the fun facts in *Elmo Asks Why*. Start by writing a question from the encyclopedia on a piece of drawing paper. Suggest that your child draws what they remember. When the picture is finished, go back into the encyclopedia and reread the answer to the why question. Add more details after rereading and then encourage your child to share the picture (and their new knowledge) with others.

Passing the crayons

Pictorial responses can also be created by "passing the crayons." Fold a piece of drawing paper into four sections. Write a "why" question from *Elmo Asks Why* in each of the four boxes. Encourage your child to pick a question and draw what they remember. Next, it is your turn. Ask your child to pass the crayon to you, select a question, and draw a response in the box. In no time, you and your child have created pictorial responses to four "why" questions from the encyclopedia. To keep the fun going, flip the paper over and create four more "why" questions about topics not included in the encyclopedia. For example, "why is the sky blue?" is answered in *Elmo Asks Why*. "Why is the grass green?" is not. Write the question "why is the grass green?" in a box, research the topic together, and then invite your child to illustrate the answer. This is a great way to extend learning after enjoying the fascinating information in the encyclopedia.

Barbara A. Marinak, PhD, is Professor and Dean of the School of Education at Mount St. Mary's University. Prior to joining the faculty at Mount St. Mary's, Dr. Marinak spent more than two decades in public education. She held a variety of leadership positions, including reading supervisor, elementary curriculum supervisor, and acting superintendent. Dr. Marinak is the 2016 recipient of the A.B. Herr Award. She is the coauthor of *No More Reading for Junk: Best Practices for Motivating Readers and Maximizing Motivation for Literacy Learning: Grades K-6*. Her research interests include reading motivation, intervention practices, and the use of informational text.

HAVE FUN!

Photo credits and acknowledgments

The publisher would like to thank the following for their kind permission to reproduce their photographs:

(Key: a-above; b-below/bottom; c-center; f-far; l-left; r-right; t-top)

14 123RF.com: Eric Isselee (crb). 25 123RF.com: Anatolii Tsekhmister / tsekhmister (clb). 38 Getty Images / iStock: ELyrae (cr). 51 Dreamstime.com: Tracy Decourcy / Rimglow (cra). 57 123RF.com: Leonello Calvetti (crb). Dorling Kindersley: Natural History Museum, London (cra). 61 123RF.com: Anthony Lister (cb). Dorling Kindersley: Natural History Museum, London (cr). 63 123RF.com: peterwaters (cra). Dreamstime.com: Katrina Brown / Tobkatrina (cr). 64 123RF.com: Bonzami Emmanuelle / cynoclub (tc). 67 Dreamstime.com: Tirrasa (c). 68 Fotolia: shama65 (crb). 71 Fotolia: Eric Isselee (clb). 74 Dreamstime.com: Eric Isselee / Isselee (clb). 76 Fotolia: Eric Isselee (cra). 80 Dreamstime.com: Chukov (crb). 85 Dreamstime.com: Vincent Giordano / Tritooth (clb). 88-89 Dreamstime.com: Sergey Kichigin / Kichigin (t). 89 Dreamstime.com: Andrey Sukhachev / Nchuprin (cl). 102 Getty Images / iStock: RTimages (ca). 109 123RF.com: Olexandr Moroz / alexandrmoroz (cb). 110 123RF.com: nerthuz (cl). 113 Dreamstime.com: Icefront (c). 114 Dreamstime.com: Digitalstormcinema (cr). 119 123RF.com: belchonock (c); Lev Kropotov (cl); Svetlana Yefimkina (br). 120 123RF.com: Nataliia Kravchuk (crb). 125 Dreamstime.com: Ali Ender Birer / Enderbirer (clb). 126 123RF.com: Vassiliy Prikhodko (tr). Dreamstime.com: Irochka (cla). 131 123RF.com: Maria Tkach (crb). Dreamstime.com: Tom Wang / Tomwang112 (crb/earthquake). 132 Dreamstime.com: Digitalbalance (cr); Viacheslav Dubrovin (c). 144 Alamy Stock Photo: Image Gap (cr). 146 Dreamstime.com: Kristina Kostova (cla). 153 123RF.com: photomelon (cr). 157 Dreamstime.com: Alexandr Kornienko (clb). 164 Dreamstime.com: Mikhail Kokhanchikov (cla); Prasit Rodphan (tr). 166 123RF.com: Channarong Yuenyong / chanchai (ca). 171 Dreamstime.com: Julin Rovagnati / Erdosain (c). Getty Images / iStock: artisteer (br). 173 Dreamstime.com: Dean Bertoncelj (tc); Oleg Dudko (tl). 181 Dreamstime.com: Paul-andr Belle-isle (clb). 183 Fotolia: Anatolii (clb). 196 Dreamstime.com: Markus Gann / Magann (cr). 204 123RF.com: Fernando Gregory Milan (cr). 206-207 Dreamstime.com: Surasak Suwanmake (cb). 209 Dreamstime.com: Konstantin Shaklein / 3dsculptor (cr)

Cover images: Front: 123RF.com: Anthony Lister cb; Dreamstime.com: Digitalstormcinema cb/ (Firetruck)

All other images © Dorling Kindersley
Cover images: © Sesame Workshop

Dorling Kindersley would like to thank Gabriela Arenas, David K. Chan, Vanessa Germosen, Akimi Gibson, Risa Greenbaum, Tanisha Isaacs, Svetlana Keselman, Lili Lampasona, Michelle Lara, Louis Henry Mitchell, Rosemary Palacios, Cat Reynolds, Meg Roth, Hayley Salmon, Susan Scheiner, Lisa Terzo, and Rosemarie Truglio at Sesame Workshop. DK also thanks Elizabeth Dowsett for fact checking, Jennette ElNaggar for proofreading, Julia March for the index, Barbara Marinak for acting as a literacy consultant, and Sakshi Saluja for assistance with picture research.

LOVE YOU, BYE!

DK | Penguin Random House

Senior Editor Tori Kosara
Senior Art Editor Lauren Adams
Senior Production Editor Jennifer Murray
Senior Production Controller Lloyd Robertson
Managing Editor Paula Regan
Managing Art Editor Jo Connor
Publishing Director Mark Searle

Written and edited for DK by Simon Beecroft
Cover and book designed for DK by Lisa Lanzarini

First American Edition, 2023
Published in the United States by DK Publishing
1745 Broadway, 20th Floor, New York, NY 10019

Page design copyright © 2023 Dorling Kindersley Limited
DK, a Division of Penguin Random House LLC
23 24 25 26 27 10 9 8 7 6 5 4 3 2 1
001–335544–Sep/2023

© 2023 Sesame Workshop®, Sesame Street®, and associated characters,
trademarks, and design elements are owned and licensed by Sesame
Workshop. All rights reserved.

All rights reserved.
Without limiting the rights under the copyright reserved above, no part of
this publication may be reproduced, stored in or introduced into a retrieval
system, or transmitted, in any form, or by any means (electronic,
mechanical, photocopying, recording, or otherwise), without the prior
written permission of the copyright owner.
Published in Great Britain by Dorling Kindersley Limited

A catalog record for this book
is available from the Library of Congress.
ISBN 978-0-7440-8460-3

DK books are available at special discounts when purchased
in bulk for sales promotions, premiums, fund-raising, or educational use.
For details, contact: DK Publishing Special Markets,
1745 Broadway, 20th Floor, New York, NY 10019
SpecialSales@dk.com

Printed and bound in China

For the curious
www.dk.com
www.sesamestreet.org

MIX
Paper | Supporting
responsible forestry
FSC™ C018179

This book was made with Forest
Stewardship Council™ certified
paper—one small step in DK's
commitment to a sustainable future.
**For more information go to
www.dk.com/our-green-pledge**